Meet The Author – Anthony Masters

What is your favourite animal?
My bantams
What is your favourite boy's name?
David
What is your favourite girl's name?
Penny
What is your favourite food?
Chinese food
What is your favourite music?
Mexican
What is your favourite h...
Canoeing

Mee... ...et Buckley

What is your favourite animal?
A cat
What is your favourite boy's name?
Ernest
What is your favourite girl's name?
Emily
What is your favourite food?
Spinach
What is your favourite music?
"There She Goes" by The La's
What is your favourite hobby?
Playing the harmonica

To Robina who brings light
With much love and thanks

Contents

Chapter 1
Waiting for Dad

"When's Dad getting back?" asked Tod.

"He'll be here soon," replied his mother, cutting up the fish.

Tod gazed out of the window and down to the beach with its piles of rotting seaweed and white fish bones. The whole coast had been reduced to a desert because it hadn't rained for months. The sea was shrinking. Now he could

hardly see the far-off line where the waves were breaking on the beach.

"Tod, you won't bring Dad back just by wishing!" his mother continued.

Tod Hunter was thirteen. His father had become a water diviner. It needed a special gift to be a water diviner and very few people had it. The hazel stick, which a water diviner carried, would shake every time he came near the precious liquid.

The government couldn't cope with the lack of water everywhere, and thousands of people had already died from thirst.

Most of the population was panicking and fighting over the small amount of water that was left. The cities had become so unsafe that Tod's father had moved his family to Cornwall.

Tod and his parents lived in a house near the dunes on what had once been a popular surfing beach. But the place was deserted now.

Tod took a last, long look. The sand stretched for miles. Near the road, the trees were dead, just blackened stumps, and there was no green anywhere. Inland there was hardly any fresh water left.

"I'm worried the Bikers might have got Dad," said Tod. "They've been searching for a water diviner."

"Don't worry. Your Dad can take care of himself," said his mother, but he knew how worried she was.

"I'm going to take the buggy out," said Tod. "I'm going to look for him."

Tod drove his beach buggy over the dunes, dust spurting up behind him, the smell of rotting seaweed in his nostrils. He was thirsty. But he was always thirsty now. They had to ration the water that Dad had found with his divining stick.

He drove the buggy towards the road. Suddenly Tod heard the sound of an engine. But it wasn't Dad's jeep. It was a bike. Tod skidded slightly and brought the buggy to a halt behind a rock. Around the corner came a Biker on a

low-slung, black machine that gleamed in the evening sun. He wore black leather and his helmet was painted with a skull and crossbones.

The Biker came to a halt, his engine spluttering. He searched in his saddlebag and brought out a bottle, taking one swig of water and then another.

As Tod watched him, the Biker stretched and yawned. Then he suddenly turned round and headed back the way he had come. I hope he doesn't run into Dad, thought Tod. The Bikers didn't obey any laws. They went around in gangs, robbing, scavenging and beating people up for their water supplies.

Tod waited until he couldn't hear the engine any longer. Then he drove home in his buggy. As he drove back, Tod glanced up at the overcast sky. He shivered in spite of the heat.

Chapter 2
A Scorcher

"I think a Scorcher's on its way," said Mum when Tod got home.

A Scorcher was a hot, dry, burning wind.

"We'd better take some supplies down to the cellar," she added.

"No sign of Dad," said Tod unhappily. It was no fun to be out when a Scorcher swept in from the sea.

"I expect he's been delayed," suggested his mother.

Tod decided not to tell her he'd seen a Biker. It would only make her more afraid than she already was.

Tod couldn't sleep that night. In his mind, he kept seeing his Dad being held prisoner by the Bikers. When Tod drifted into a doze he dreamt that Dad was being forced to use his divining stick. He could hear him yelling, "Help me, Tod! You've got to help me."

In his dream, Tod tried to run towards him, but his feet kept sinking into the sand.

He woke with a start and got up, hurrying into his parents' room. But only his mother was there.

"Where's Dad?"

"Still not home." She was looking out of the window. "The Scorcher's coming now."

Tod gazed at the steel grey sky. The scorching winds were the result of changes in the weather pattern. They were so hot and dry that they could burn away human flesh. He could already hear the rattling, rasping gusts as the Scorcher approached.

"I've put everything we need in the cellar," said his mother. "Let's get down there. Dad will be OK," she told Tod, as they sat in the old armchairs and watched the sand spill through tiny cracks in the cellar wall. "He'll have taken shelter somewhere."

If he's not been kidnapped by the Bikers, thought Tod. But out loud he said, trying to keep calm, "He'll be home soon."

Soon they could only just hear each other speak as the Scorcher blasted the beach. The cellar was incredibly hot and his mother told Tod to drink some water from the jar on the floor. They were both sweating.

"Go on, Mum," insisted Tod. "You have some water too."

The Scorcher slowly blew itself out. When the screaming sound had gone, they both went up the stairs. The house was undamaged, but there were piles of red-hot sand against the front door. Then Tod suddenly heard a roaring sound.

"Surely the Scorcher can't be coming back ..." began Mum.

But Tod had already seen the Bikers speeding across the dunes towards them, looking like a pack of black vultures.

Chapter 3
Unwanted Visitors

"Quick, get out the back, Mum. The Bikers are on their way. We can hide in the wood," shouted Tod.

"Why are they coming here?" his mother gasped.

"To see if they can find any water records," replied Tod.

"Dad keeps them in the safe," his mother reminded him.

"They could blow it open," Tod suggested.

They gazed at each other, suddenly knowing what must have happened.

"That means they've got him, doesn't it?" hissed his mother.

"Maybe," shrugged Tod.

"If they haven't, why are they coming here?" she asked.

"We haven't got time to talk. Let's go."

Tod and his mother ran outside and into a wood of skeleton trees with blackened branches.

As they crouched down they heard the Bikers coming closer to the house. Then they stopped, switched off their engines and there was a long silence.

"What's going on?" hissed Mum.

"I can't see."

Then they both heard the sound of the front door being kicked in. They waited for what seemed a very long time until a heavy dragging sound came from the porch, followed by a soft thump.

"That's the safe," whispered Tod.

There was another long delay. Then they heard a loud bang.

"That *was* the safe. They've blown it up."

Tod wondered if the Bikers had tortured his father and had only come to the house because he wouldn't talk.

Then they both heard the revving of motorbike engines.

"They might have left someone on guard," said Tod. "I'm going to creep up to the house. You stay here. There's no point in us both getting caught."

Tod approached the house very slowly in case anyone was waiting on the porch. The front door was swinging off its hinges, and the blown-open safe lay on the sand.

Tod was suddenly furious. How could the Bikers invade their home like this? Then he wondered what they might have done to his Dad.

"I thought I told you to wait in the wood," he muttered as his mother arrived.

"Don't boss me around," she replied angrily. "Just look at all this mess! I've had enough. We'll have to go and find your father."

"We?" he asked.

"Yes. You go north and I'll go south," his mother told him. "We've no idea where he is."

"Biker City?"

"Could be," she said.

"Then I'm going south," insisted Tod. "I've got the buggy and that's faster then your old Ford."

"You'll be careful," she begged.

"We've *got* to find him, Mum."

"What can either of us do against the Bikers?" asked his mother hopelessly.

Chapter 4
Tod Alone

Tod and his mother split up when they reached the main road. They had filled their rucksacks with as much food and water as they could carry.

"You won't take any silly risks, will you?" said his mother.

But the time for keeping their true feelings hidden was over. "It's all a risk, Mum. You know that."

Her eyes filled with tears as she got into her battered old car. "I know," she said. "God be with you."

Tod was shaken. His mother hadn't said that to him in years. Not since their old home had burnt down in a Scorcher and the family had been forced to search for somewhere else to live.

Tod watched the battered Ford disappear, his mother's hand waving until she was out of sight.

Then he revved up his beach buggy and began to speed over the dunes. Tod drove over miles of deserted beach, passing the skeletons of stranded fish and even a large whale.

Then he saw a dark shape. As he drove nearer, Tod realised that it was a water tower which stood in front of him. The familiar skull and crossbones was crudely painted on the side in red. Tod knew he would be crazy to go any nearer. He would have to hide the buggy in the dunes and walk. The midday sun was blazing down on a rusting heap of old trucks, buses, cars and even a few railway carriages.

Tod crouched behind a pile of rock. Where had the Bikers gone? Then he thought he heard something move behind him. A few metres away, piled up in the dunes, were a number of empty oil drums. Had the noise come from there? Or had he been mistaken?

He couldn't see anything, but the white ball of a sun was gleaming so brightly that Tod was almost blinded. He turned back and gazed despairingly at the rusty scrapyard that was the Bikers' home. Where were they? And, most

important of all, what had they done with his father?

Then a solid weight landed on his shoulders, pushing Tod down into the burning hot sand. Tod rolled over, kicking out, sending his attacker sprawling on his back. Then Tod jumped to his feet and threw himself on top of the boy, who was dressed in the leather gear of the Bikers. Tod landed with his knees on the boy's chest and held down his arms. The boy struggled, but Tod was too strong for him.

"Where are the Bikers?" he demanded.

"Don't know," the boy replied.

Tod pressed his knees into the boy's shoulders and he howled with pain.

"Where *are* they?"

"Dunno," replied the boy again.

"You've got to tell me!"

"I won't."

Tod thought fast. The boy was looking terrified. Did he think he was going to kill him?

"Do you want some water?" Tod asked.

"You got some?" The boy's eyes narrowed and Tod could see from his dust-caked lips that he hadn't drunk for some time. Maybe a long time.

"A couple of bottles," Tod told him.

"As much as that?" exclaimed the boy.

"What's your name?"

"Billy." He looked up at Tod. He clearly did not trust him. "How do I know you've got water?"

"You'll have to trust me."

"Don't make me laugh."

Tod got up. "All right. Follow me."

Billy scrambled to his feet.

Tod pulled a bottle of water out of his rucksack. "I'll trade you half of this."

"What for?" asked Billy.

"You've got to tell me where they've taken my Dad."

Billy gazed at the water, licking his lips, hardly able to control himself.

"Let's have the water first," he insisted.

"No way." Tod shook the bottle and Billy gasped as he heard the wonderful sound of the water sloshing about inside.

"They're down at the old tin mine. It's on the other side of the city. They found your Dad there waggling his hazel stick."

"Water divining, you mean?"

"He thought he was safe because we'd been away on a raid."

"Why did they leave you behind?"

"I nicked some water from the tower. Not much. Just a few drops, but they went crazy. So they left me on guard."

"Some guard," said Tod with scorn in his voice. "Now give me directions."

"You go straight on, right through the city. There's a sign to the old tin mine." Billy paused. "Now what about that water?"

Tod passed him the bottle. "That's enough," he said.

But Billy went on drinking. Tod grabbed the bottle. After a slight struggle, Billy reluctantly passed it back.

"One thing," Billy said.

"What's that?" asked Tod.

"Don't grass me up. They'll kill me."

Tod collected his beach buggy and began to drive through the city. When he glanced back he saw that Billy was watching him. He looked lonely. Tod felt almost sorry for him. But he had to find the old tin mine. He had to find his Dad.

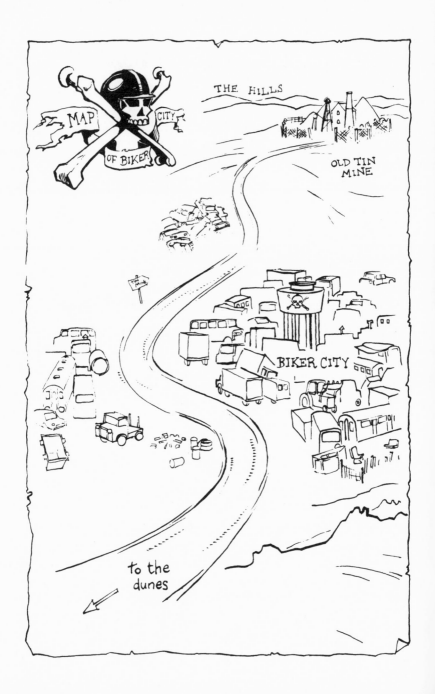

Chapter 5
A Cry in the Dark

There was a hot wind coming off the distant sea. It wasn't nearly as bad as a Scorcher, but it was still blowing strongly. It picked up fine grains of sand and hurled them into Tod's eyes, which began to sting badly. Then, with relief, at the very end of Biker City he saw a faded sign which said TIN MINE.

Tod drove on, arriving at a pile of wrecked cars which gave him some cover. The heat was intense, but what really worried him was the chance that he might meet the returning Bikers at any moment.

Tod gazed ahead, listening hard, but there was only silence. Scraggy gulls hovered over the bare fields which stretched up to the rocky hills beyond Biker City.

Slowly he drove on again, and suddenly saw the shabby buildings of the old tin mine. Parked outside were dozens of motorbikes. Trying not to skid or screech his brakes, Tod drove back the way he had come until he reached the pile of wrecked cars. He hid the buggy behind them. Then Tod jumped down on to the sand and ran back to the mine again, checking whether the bright yellow beach buggy could be seen or not.

Unfortunately one mudguard was sticking out from behind the cars. Then he saw the

Bikers coming out of the mine. Tod flung himself into a shallow ditch and burrowed into a pile of sand. All the time he was worrying about the yellow mudguard of the buggy that the Bikers were bound to notice. Then they would come searching for him.

Tod lay as low as he could as the Bikers passed him, all travelling at high speed. Dust spurted up, falling on him in a low, choking cloud. When he raised his head, Tod saw them riding away, bent low over their handlebars. Gulls flew behind the Bikers, as if they were following a fishing boat and hoped someone might throw them something to eat.

The Bikers had been going too fast to notice the buggy, and Tod got to his feet with relief. He went back behind the pile of cars and hid the buggy properly.

Then Tod began to walk slowly back to the tin mine, looking out for danger all the time.

When he reached the tumbledown buildings there seemed to be no one around. But the silence was frightening, making his heart pound. Tod moved on, heading towards the mine shaft which was open. He gazed down into the darkness. What was he going to do?

Tod lay down on his stomach and stuck his head down into the darkness of the shaft. He felt exposed. Billy had jumped him when he had been off-guard. He had been able to deal with him, because he was so much stronger than Billy. Tod knew he would be no match against a real Biker.

"Dad?" he yelled. "Are you down there? Can you hear me, Dad?"

The silence was like an invisible wall. Maybe his father wasn't down there anyway.

Tod tried again.

"Dad!" he bellowed. "Can you hear me?"

The echo of his voice seemed to thunder up from the mine shaft and out into Biker City.

Then he heard a faint cry.

Tod shouted down the shaft again and this time he was sure he heard his father's voice.

"Dad! Hang on. I'm coming down."

Tod knew the old tin mines weren't that deep. The miners had been lowered in the cage that was rotting away beside him. Luckily there was an escape ladder as well. Then a muffled cry was repeated over and over again, but Tod couldn't make out the words.

Without waiting any longer he stood up, grabbed the top of the ladder and began to climb down into the musty-smelling darkness.

Chapter 6
Descent into Darkness

Tod began to feel more confident as he went down, picking up speed until he came to a sudden halt. He realised he'd run out of ladder. There was a sheer drop beneath him.

If only he had thought to bring a torch. There was darkness all round Tod and he could only just make out the dim light at the top of the shaft. He gazed down fearfully. Suddenly,

the feeble light of a torch whose batteries were running out gleamed up at him. Now he knew he had found his Dad at last.

"They've chopped off the ladder so they can keep me prisoner down here."

"I'll jump," called down Tod.

"Go back," his father pleaded. "There's no way you can help me."

"You know I'd never leave you down there."

"You'll only trap yourself as well. Be sensible. Go back home. I'll sort this out," said his father.

"I'm coming down, Dad. I'm going to jump."

"Wait!" His father seemed to have given up trying to stop him. "Let me get into the right position."

"What for?"

"Catching you."

For a moment Tod hesitated. Suppose he broke a leg? They would both be trapped down there in the darkness.

But what else could he do? He *had* to jump.

"Ready?" asked his father.

"I'm coming. Now."

Tod let go and pushed himself away from the ladder.

The fall seemed to take a long, long time. Then he felt a terrific thump as he landed on his father's chest, his arms around his waist. They both fell on to the ground and he heard a gasp of pain.

Then Tod realised he was lying on top of his father who still had his arms around his waist, hugging him tightly. Tod rolled clear and scrambled to his feet. Nothing hurt. Nothing was broken. He picked up the torch and shone the faint beam on his father who was getting to his feet much more slowly.

"You OK, Dad?" Tod asked.

"Just a bit winded. You all right?" his father replied.

"I'm fine. What happened?"

"I was water divining down here and the Bikers found me. They said I had to work for them, but I refused," explained Dad.

Tod could see that his father's face was badly bruised.

"They beat you up!"

"I wasn't going to give in. When I refused to co-operate they chopped off the last part of the ladder so I couldn't get out. They've gone again, using a rope they had with them, but they said they'd be coming back tomorrow morning."

"What are they going to do then?" asked Tod fearfully.

"They said I was to think things over. If I don't agree to find water for them, they'll kill me."

"But you haven't found any yet."

"That's the trouble. I have," said Dad.

Chapter 7
A Dangerous Discovery

The torch beam was getting fainter all the time as Tod followed his father. Then he came to a sudden halt and picked up his water divining stick from the floor. Directly he pointed it at the wall, the stick began to move with a will of its own.

"There's water on the other side. An underground stream, I think."

"How do we get at it?" asked Tod.

"I've got a couple of heavy hammers. The rock's thin and cracked. If we work really hard we might be able to get through. The two of us will make a difference."

"Aren't you glad I tracked you down?" Tod said.

"Your mother will be out of her mind with worry."

"She'll still be searching," Tod replied.

Tod could see the tears in his father's eyes as he said, "Let's get stuck in."

Tod and his father hammered away at the rock for over an hour before they got anywhere.

"I'm sure I can smell water," his father said.

But Tod couldn't smell anything except the musty dankness of the tunnel. What's more the hole they had made seemed very small. He felt depressed and tired out as they began to hammer away again. Tod was thankful that the face of his watch lit up in the dark. The torch had long since given out.

"It's after midnight. How much longer are we going to take?" asked Tod.

"We've got to work faster. The Bikers will be back at first light," replied his father.

Chapter 8
Swim for your Life!

After a couple of hours of numbing, hard work, a large section of rock suddenly fell inwards and there was the sound of a splash.

"We made it," croaked his father. "That must have been a weak seam. We can both get through."

He was right and Tod felt his spirits rise suddenly.

As Dad began to scramble into the watery darkness, they both heard a noise further back in the tunnel.

"You said they'd come at dawn, Dad," hissed Tod.

"They must need a drink badly," his father replied.

The water was round their knees as they clambered into the dark space. Then a sudden beam of light cut into the darkness.

"Stop!" yelled a Biker.

Then Tod heard one of them say, "There's water. Precious water." His voice broke. "We can drink."

"Keep going, Dad," urged Tod. "We've got to go wherever the stream takes us."

But the water was already up to his waist. Then Tod banged his head.

"It's a dead end," he gasped.

"Not quite. The stream's going underground," his father told him.

More strong beams lit up the tunnel. By their light they could see that the water was flowing under a rocky shelf.

"We're finished," whispered Tod.

"There's a chance the stream might flow out into a cave."

"Let's dive," said Tod. "The Bikers don't need you now. They'll kill us both if we go back."

He looked at the narrow gap between the stream and the rock. How long could they go on swimming underwater without breathing? Three minutes?

"I'll go first," said Tod.

Once he was caught in the current, Tod was thrown from one side of the underground stream to the other, hitting the rocky sides of the tunnel again and again. He had taken a deep breath when he dived, but already his lungs were hurting. How far *would* they have to swim before they escaped?

Chapter 9
Where to Now?

Tod knew he was going to drown. He couldn't last out any longer and all he could see was a red mist. He thought his lungs were going to burst. Mum was going to be left alone, he thought sadly. She'd never see either of them again. Then, just as Tod was beginning to pass out, he felt himself being sucked forward. Suddenly his lungs were full of glorious air and the current became gentle, spinning him around. He bumped hard into his father as he, too, was pushed out of the tunnel. They stood gasping, waist-deep in the water in a huge cavern that was half lit with a pale light from above.

"It's a miracle," wheezed Dad.

They dragged themselves out and lay on their backs, filling their lungs with the wonderful air.

The light from a split in the rock was strong enough for them to see that they were covered in cuts and their bodies felt badly bruised.

"Where are we?" asked Tod.

"This must be the Hollow Hill," his father told him.

"I thought that was just a story."

"Now we know it's for real."

They both turned over on their stomachs and leant over the stream, drinking until, at last, they'd satisfied their thirsts.

"It's a pity the Bikers found the water," said Tod.

"They'll try and control the water rights and that could start a civil war. We're going to have to move on," said his father.

"Where to?"

"Devon, maybe. There are not so many Bikers there."

Suddenly the sound of an engine filled the cave and they both hurriedly crouched down behind a rock. We should have realised the Bikers would know their own city, thought Tod.

"Let's get back in the water." He was just about to move when his father grabbed him.

"There's no time. Besides, that's not the engine note of a bike. It sounds more like your beach buggy."

Tod and his father were amazed to see Billy at the wheel and Mum sitting beside him. The buggy bumped over the rocky floor towards them, then squealed to a halt. Tod leapt up angrily, clenching his fists.

"What do you think you're doing? Nicking my buggy and kidnapping my ..."

"He didn't do anything of the kind," snapped Tod's mother. "Billy said he knew where you were, but didn't dare go near the shaft because of the Bikers. Then he found the cave entrance. Now why are you both so wet?"

"It's a long story ..." Tod replied.

"Let me get at that water." Billy sprinted over and drank his fill from the stream, while the Hunter family hugged each other.

Then Billy looked up.

"My lot are going to kill me for this."

There was a long pause. Then Tod said slowly, "So why don't you come with us? We're moving on to Devon."

"That's a great idea," said Mum. She glanced at her husband and he nodded.

"If that's really OK by you, Tod," his father said.

"It's OK by me," Tod replied.

He was sure there were tears in Billy's eyes.

Great reads – no problem!

Barrington Stoke books are:

Great stories – funny, scary or exciting – and all by the best writers around!

No hassle – fast reads with no boring bits, and a brilliant story that you can't put down.

Short – the perfect size for a fast, fun read.

We use our own font and paper to make it easier for dyslexic people to read our books too. And we ask readers like you to check every book before it's published.

That way, we know for sure that every Barrington Stoke book is a great read for everyone.

Check out www.barringtonstoke.co.uk for more info about Barrington Stoke and our books!

You do not need to read this page – just get on with the book!

First published in 1999 in Great Britain by
Barrington Stoke Ltd
18 Walker St, Edinburgh, EH3 7LP

www.barringtonstoke.co.uk

This edition published 2001

Reprinted 2001 (twice), 2002 (twice), 2003, 2005, 2007

ISBN: 978-1-90226-087-7

Printed in Great Britain by Bell & Bain Ltd

Tod in Biker City

by

Anthony Masters

Illustrated by Harriet Buckley